SHORT TALES
Fables

The FOX and the GRAPES

Adapted by Christopher E. Long
Illustrated by John Cboins

magic wagon

Published by Magic Wagon, a division of the ABDO Group, 8000 West 78th Street, Edina, Minnesota, 55439. Copyright © 2010 by Abdo Consulting Group, Inc. International copyrights reserved in all countries. All rights reserved. No part of this book may be reproduced in any form without written permission from the publisher.

Short Tales ™ is a trademark and logo of Magic Wagon.

Printed in the United States of America, North Mankato, Minnesota.
092009
012010

PRINTED ON RECYCLED PAPER

Adapted Text by Christopher E. Long
Illustrations by John Cboins
Colors by John Cboins
Edited by Stephanie Hedlund
Interior Layout by Kristen Fitzner Denton
Book Design and Packaging by Shannon Eric Denton

Library of Congress Cataloging-in-Publication Data

Long, Christopher E.
  The fox and the grapes / adapted by Christopher E. Long ; illustrated by John Cboins.
     p. cm. -- (Short tales. Fables)
  ISBN 978-1-60270-553-1
  [1. Fables. 2. Folklore.] I. Cboins, John, ill. II. Aesop. III. Title.
  PZ8.2.L65Fo 2010
  398.2--dc22
  [E]

                                          2008032304

Fox slept in the cool shade.

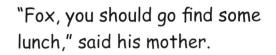

"Fox, you should go find some lunch," said his mother.

"Someone will bring me something to eat," Fox said.

"But your brother is finding his own food," said his mother.

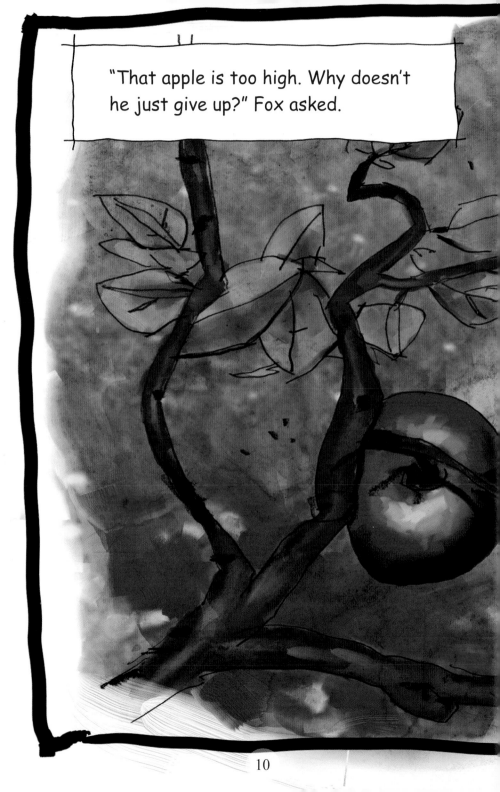

"That apple is too high. Why doesn't he just give up?" Fox asked.

"Because nothing is sweeter than something you work to get," his mother said.

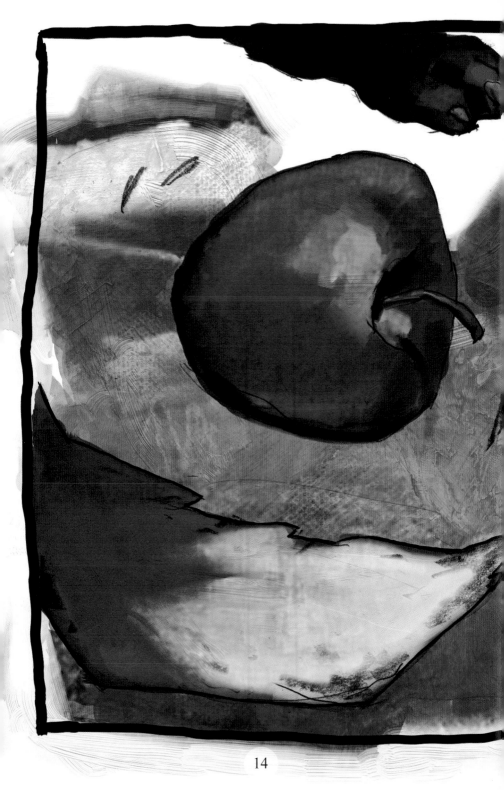

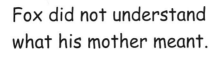

Fox did not understand
what his mother meant.

"Brother Fox, have you had lunch?" Fox's brother asked.

"No, I haven't," Fox said.

Fox had known someone would bring him something to eat.

Later that day, Fox got hungry.

23

He walked into the forest to find his family.

"Those grapes sure do look good,"
Fox said.

Fox jumped high, but he could not reach the grapes.

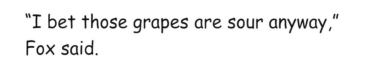

"I bet those grapes are sour anyway,"
Fox said.

The moral of the story is:

It's easy to despise what you cannot have.